*TIMELESS SHAKESPEARE*

THE MERCHANT OF VENICE

William Shakespeare

– ADAPTED BY –

Emily Hutchinson

SADDLEBACK
EDUCATIONAL PUBLISHING

TIMELESS SHAKESPEARE

Hamlet

Julius Caesar

King Lear

Macbeth

The Merchant of Venice

A Midsummer Night's Dream

Othello

Romeo and Juliet

The Tempest

Twelfth Night

SADDLEBACK
EDUCATIONAL PUBLISHING
www.sdlback.com

ISBN-13: 978-1-61651-106-7
ISBN-10: 1-61651-106-0
eBook: 978-1-60291-840-5

Printed in the United States of America
15 14 13 12 11   1 2 3 4 5

| Contents |

– BACKGROUND –

Bassanio asks his friend Antonio for money to woo the heiress Portia. Antonio borrows the money from Shylock, a Jewish moneylender. Because Shylock hates all Christians—and Antonio in particular—he foregoes his usual interest. Instead, he asks for a pound of Antonio's flesh if the money is not repaid in three months. Then Antonio's business goes bad. He loses all his money and is unable to repay Shylock. Now even angrier toward Christians because of his daughter's elopement with one, Shylock wants his pound of flesh. All looks hopeless until Portia shows up at the trial, dressed as a judge. Will she be clever enough to render a fair judgment and thus save poor Antonio's life?

– CAST OF CHARACTERS –

THE DUKE OF VENICE, PRINCE OF MOROCCO, and **PRINCE OF ARAGON** Suitors to Portia

ANTONIO A merchant of Venice

BASSANIO Antonio's friend

GRATIANO, SOLANIO, and **SALERIO** Friends of Antonio and Bassanio

LORENZO In love with Jessica

SHYLOCK A Jewish moneylender

TUBAL Another Jew, and friend of Shylock

LANCELOT GOBBO Servant to Shylock and later Bassanio

OLD GOBBO Lancelot's father

LEONARDO Servant to Bassanio

BALTHAZAR and **STEPHANO** Servants to Portia

PORTIA A wealthy lady of Belmont

NERISSA Portia's waiting-maid

JESSICA Shylock's daughter

OFFICERS OF THE COURT OF JUSTICE, a **JAILER, SERVANTS,** and **ATTENDANTS**

ACT 1

| Scene 1 |

A wharf in Venice, Italy, in the sixteenth century.
*Antonio is talking to his friends **Salerio** and **Solanio**.*

ANTONIO *(sighing)*: I don't know why
I'm so sad. This mood wearies me.
You say it wearies you, too.
But just how I caught it, found it,
  or came by it,
I do not know. I feel so sad,
I hardly even know myself.

SALERIO: Your mind is tossing on the ocean.
(pointing toward the sea) It's out there,
Where your ships with their billowing sails
Lord it over the common working boats.

SOLANIO: Believe me, if I had taken the risks
That you have, I would be worried, too.
Anything that put my investments at risk
Would make me sad.

SALERIO: As I blew on my hot soup to cool it,
I'd catch a chill when I thought
What harm a strong wind might do at sea.
As I looked at the sand in an hourglass,
I'd think of shallow waters and sandbanks

And see one of my ships stuck in the sand.
Every time I went to church, the holy
  stones
Would make me think of dangerous rocks.
They'd only have to touch my delicate
  ship
To scatter all her spices into the sea
And clothe the wild waters with my silks!
One moment I'd be rich—
And the next I'd be worth nothing.
How miserable I would be
If such a thing happened!
You can't fool me. I know Antonio must
Be worrying about his merchandise.

ANTONIO: Believe me, that's not it. I'm lucky.
My investments are not all in one ship
Or all in one place. Nor is all my money
At risk at this time. So my merchandise
Is not what is making me sad.

SOLANIO *(teasing)*: Why, then, you must
Be in love!

ANTONIO *(protesting)*: Not at all!

SOLANIO: Not in love, either? Then let us say
You are sad because you are not merry.
And, if you wanted to, you could laugh.

*(**Bassanio, Lorenzo,** and **Gratiano** enter.)*
Here comes Bassanio, your noble kinsman.

Gratiano and Lorenzo are with him.
(seeing his chance to leave) Farewell!
We'll leave you now with better company.

SALERIO *(also seeing his chance)*:
I would have stayed to cheer you up
If worthier friends had not stopped me.

ANTONIO: That's good of you, but I take it
Your own business calls you.
This gives you the chance to leave.

SALERIO *(to the newcomers)*: Good morning!

BASSANIO *(warmly)*: Gentlemen both!
When shall we have a laugh together, eh?
You're almost strangers! Must it be so?

SALERIO *(eager to get away)*: Yes, yes. We'll get
together one of these days.

*(**Salerio** and **Solanio** exit.)*

LORENZO: Bassanio, now that you have
Found Antonio, we will leave you.
Remember that we're meeting for dinner.

BASSANIO: I'll be there!

GRATIANO: You don't look well, Antonio.
You let things get you down.
Don't worry so much. Believe me,
You don't seem like yourself lately.

ANTONIO: I take the world as it is, Gratiano,
A stage, where every man must play a part,
And mine a sad one.

GRATIANO: Let me play the fool, then.
  Let mirth and laughter give me wrinkles,
  And let my emotions get heated with wine
  Rather than let my heart cool with sighs.
  Why should a warmblooded man
  Act like a stone-cold statue of his
    grandfather?
  I tell you what, Antonio—
  And I speak out of friendship—
  Some men have faces that never change.
  They stay still, hoping to be thought of as
  Wise, serious, and important.
    Antonio, I know men whose reputation
  For being wise is based on saying nothing.
  I am very sure that, if they would speak,
  They would prove themselves fools.
  I'll tell you more about this another time.
  But don't go fishing for this fake reputation
  With melancholy as your bait, Lorenzo.
  *(to Antonio)***:** Farewell for now.
  I'll end my speech after dinner.

LORENZO: Yes, we'll see you at dinnertime.
  I must be one of those silent wise men,
  For Gratiano never lets me speak.

GRATIANO: Be my friend two more years—
  You'll forget the sound of your own voice!

ANTONIO *(to Gratiano)***:** I guess I'd better start
  talking, then.

GRATIANO: If you like. Silence is only good
  In dried ox tongues and young maids!

*(**Gratiano** and **Lorenzo** exit.)*

ANTONIO: What do you think of that?

BASSANIO *(laughing)*: He talks more trash
  Than any man in Venice! Any truth
  Gratiano speaks is like two grains of wheat
  Hidden in two bushels.
  Look all day, and when you find them,
  They are not worth the search!

ANTONIO: Well, tell me now,
  What lady takes your fancy?
  You promised to tell me about her today.

BASSANIO *(serious now)*: Antonio, you know
  Only too well that I've been spending
  My inheritance by living beyond my means.
  I'm not angry about having to cut back—
  But my main goal is to pay the great debts
    that my extravagant living has cost me.
  I owe the most to you, Antonio, in money
  And in friendship. Because we are friends,
  I dare to speak freely about my plans to
  Get clear of all the debts I owe.

ANTONIO: Bassanio, tell me everything.
  If your plan is honorable—as you are—
  Be assured that my purse, my person, and
  All my resources are open to you.

BASSANIO: In my schooldays,
If I lost one arrow,
I shot another in the same way. I watched
Its flight carefully to see where the first fell.
By risking both, I often found both.
 I tell this childhood story
Because my new plan is very similar.
I owe you much and—blame my youth—
What I owe is lost.
But if you would shoot another arrow
The same way you shot the first,
I'll either find both or bring the second one
Back to you again. Then I'll gratefully
Stand by the first debt I owed you.

ANTONIO: You know me well enough.
By doubting that I'd help you, you hurt me
More than if you had wasted all I have.
Just tell me what to do, and I'll do it!

BASSANIO: There is a rich heiress
In Belmont. She is beautiful and virtuous.
Sometimes I have received silent messages
From her eyes. Her name is Portia.
The world is not ignorant of her worth,
For the four winds blow in famous suitors
From every coast. Antonio, if only I had
The money to compete with these suitors,
I'm convinced I could win her hand.

ANTONIO: You know that my wealth is tied up

In cargoes at sea. I do not have the cash,
Nor do I have anything to sell right now.
So go to Venice. See what my credit can do.
Stretch it to the limit to finance your trip
To Belmont and the fair Portia. Go right
   now
And ask around, and so will I. See
   where money is to be had.
Borrow it on my credit or good name.
Either way, it comes out the same.

*(**Bassanio** and **Antonio** exit.)*

| Scene 2 |

*The hall at Portia's house at Belmont. **Portia** is talking with her maid, **Nerissa**.*

PORTIA: Honestly, Nerissa, my little body is weary of this great world.

NERISSA: You would be better off, dear lady, if you had as much misery as you have good fortune. As I see it, those who have too much are as miserable as those who have too little. Excess gives you white hair and makes you old before your time! Moderation leads to a longer life.

PORTIA: Good sentences, and well-said.

NERISSA: They'd be better if well-followed.

PORTIA: If doing were as easy as knowing what to do, poor men's cottages would be palaces. It is a good preacher who follows his own instructions. I'd rather teach twenty how to act than be one of the twenty to follow my own teaching! The brain might try to control the emotions, but a hot temper leaps over a cold rule. Youth ignores good advice because it's a handicap. But all this reasoning won't help me choose a husband. Oh, dear! *(sighing)* That word "choose"! I may neither choose whom I like, nor refuse whom I dislike. So the will of a living daughter is curbed by the will of a dead father. Isn't it unfair, Nerissa, that I can neither choose nor refuse?

NERISSA: Your father was very virtuous, and good men are often inspired on their deathbeds. The lottery he set up is a worthy idea. Given a choice of gold, silver, or lead—with you as the prize for the correct choice—only the right man will choose correctly. How do you feel about the princely suitors who have already come to seek your hand?

PORTIA: Please name them. And as you do so, I will describe them for you. Then you can guess by my descriptions how I feel about each of them.

NERISSA: First there is the prince from Naples.

PORTIA: Oh, yes, that colt! He does nothing but talk about his horse. He brags that he can shoe the beast himself. I suspect that his mother once had an affair with a blacksmith!

NERISSA: Then there is the Count Palatine.

PORTIA: He does nothing but frown, as if to say, "If you won't marry me, choose someone else!" He listens to jokes and never smiles. I'm sure he'll be the weeping prophet when he grows old, being so full of sadness in his youth. I would rather be married to a skull than to either of these!

NERISSA: What do you say about the French lord, Monsieur Le Bon?

PORTIA: Honestly, I know it's a sin to be a mocker—but him! I would be happy if he hated me, for I could never return his love.

NERISSA: And the young English baron?

PORTIA: You know I never speak to him. He doesn't understand me, and I don't understand him. He speaks neither Latin,

French, nor Italian. And you know that my English is not good. He looks manly enough—but who could converse with a dummy? And how oddly he dresses! I think he bought his vest in Italy, his stockings in France, his hat in Germany, and his behavior everywhere!

NERISSA: What about the young German?

PORTIA: I dislike him in the morning when he is sober, and loathe him in the afternoon when he is drunk. When he is at his best, he is less than a man. When he is at his worst, he is little better than a beast.

NERISSA: What if he offers to choose and he chooses the right chest? You would be going against your father's will if you refused to marry him.

PORTIA: Therefore, to prevent the worst, I ask you to set a large glass of Rhine wine on the wrong casket. He'd be tempted to choose that one even if the devil were hidden inside it. I would do anything, Nerissa, before I would marry a sponge!

NERISSA: Dear lady, you need not worry about having any of these lords. They have told me what they have decided. Unless you can be won by some method other than

your father's device of the caskets, they
will return to their homes and trouble
you no more.

PORTIA: I'll die a virgin unless I'm courted
according to my father's will! I'm glad
this group of suitors is so reasonable.
There's not one of them whose absence
I don't find pleasurable.

NERISSA: Do you remember, dear lady, a suitor
from Venice?

PORTIA: Yes, yes! It was Bassanio. At least,
I think that was his name.

NERISSA: True, madam. Of all the men my
foolish eyes have ever looked upon, he
was the most deserving of a fair lady.

PORTIA: I remember him well. Yes, Bassanio is
worthy of your praise.
*(A **servant** enters.)* Well, what news?

SERVANT: The four strangers are looking
for you, madam, to say goodbye.
A messenger has arrived from a fifth—
the Prince of Morocco. He announces
that the prince will be here tonight.

PORTIA: If I can greet the fifth as eagerly
as I can bid the other four farewell,
I'll be glad to see him. Come, Nerissa.
(to the servant): Go on ahead.

(sighing) We no sooner shut the gate on
one wooer than another knocks at it!

*(**They** exit.)*

| Scene 3 |

*A street in Venice, outside Shylock's house. **Bassanio**
and **Shylock** are discussing a loan.*

SHYLOCK: You want 3,000 ducats . . .

BASSANIO: Yes, sir. For three months.
Antonio will guarantee it. Will you do it?

SHYLOCK *(thinking aloud)*: 3,000 ducats for three
months. Antonio will guarantee it. . . .

BASSANIO: What do you say?

SHYLOCK: Antonio is a good man.

BASSANIO: Have you heard differently?

SHYLOCK *(laughing)*: Oh, no, no, no, no!
When I say "a good man," you must
understand that I mean he is good for
the money. But his wealth is at risk.
He has merchant ships going to
Tripoli, the Indies, Mexico, and
England—plus other foreign risks.
But ships are only wood. Sailors are
only men. There are land rats and water
rats, land thieves and water thieves.
Pirates, I mean. And then there are

the dangers of waters, winds, and rocks!
Even so, the man is sound. You say 3,000
ducats? I think I can do it.

BASSANIO: Be assured that you can.

SHYLOCK: I will be assured. What's the latest
news about Antonio's investments? And
who is this coming?

(Antonio enters.)

BASSANIO: It's Antonio.

SHYLOCK *(aside)*: He looks like a
Fawning innkeeper!
I hate him because he is a Christian.
But I hate him even more because he
Humbly lends out money free of charge,
Bringing down the rate of interest
Here in Venice. If I can catch him unaware,
  I'll pay off old scores very well.
He hates us Jews. He speaks against me,
My deals, and my hard-earned profit,
Which he calls "usury." May my tribe
Be cursed if I ever forgive him!

BASSANIO: Shylock, are you listening?

SHYLOCK: I am figuring out my assets.
  By the near guess of my memory,
  I cannot instantly raise up the full amount
  Of 3,000 ducats. But what of that?
  Tubal, a wealthy fellow-Hebrew,

Will help me out. But, wait, I forgot—
When do you plan to pay it back?
(bowing to Antonio) Don't worry, sir,
We were just speaking about you.

ANTONIO: Shylock—although I never
Lend or borrow money with high
interest—
I'll make an exception to help my friend.
*(to Bassanio)***:** Does he know how much
you want?

SHYLOCK: Yes, yes—3,000 ducats.

ANTONIO: And for three months.

SHYLOCK: I had forgotten. Yes, three months.
You did tell me. Well, then.
Your guarantee . . . let me see . . .
But listen. I thought you said
You never lend or borrow for profit.

ANTONIO: I never do.

SHYLOCK: When Jacob grazed
His Uncle Laban's sheep—

ANTONIO *(impatiently)***:** What of him?
Did he take interest?

SHYLOCK: No, he didn't.
Not what you would call direct interest.
Here's what he did. He and Laban agreed
That all the newborn lambs with stripes
And markings would go to Jacob as wages.

When the ewes and the rams were mating,
The skillful shepherd peeled some sticks
And stuck them up in sight of the ewes.
   At this point, the ewes conceived.
And so, at lambing time, they dropped
Lambs with stripes and other markings.
Those lambs were Jacob's.
This was a way to profit, and he was blessed.
Profit is a blessing if men don't steal for it.

ANTONIO: Jacob was involved in speculation.
(smiling at Shylock's ignorance) The sticks
Had nothing to do with the outcome.
Did you tell us this to justify profit?
Or are you claiming that your
Gold and silver are like ewes and rams?

SHYLOCK: I can't tell, I make it breed as fast!

ANTONIO: Note this, Bassanio. The devil
Can quote Scripture for his own purposes.
An evil man who quotes the Bible
   is like a villain with a smiling face
Or a good apple rotten at the core.
Oh, how attractive falsehood can seem!
Well, Shylock, how about the loan?

SHYLOCK: Antonio, many a time you have
Criticized me for my moneylending.
I've taken it with a patient shrug,
For suffering is the badge of our tribe.
You call me an infidel, a cutthroat dog,

And spit on my Jewish garments.
All for using what is my own!
Well, now it appears you need my help.
You come to me, and you say, "Shylock,
We'd like some money." You, who spat
On my beard and kicked me as you would
Kick a strange dog out of your house!
What should I say to you?
"Does a dog have money? Is it possible
That a dog could lend 3,000 ducats?" Or
Should I bow low and say humbly,
"Fair sir, you spat on me last Wednesday.
You spurned me on such-and-such a day.
Another time you called me a dog.
For this, I'll lend you this much money"?

ANTONIO: I am likely to call you so again,
And spit on you and kick you, too!
If you will lend this money, don't lend it
As if to a friend. What kind of friendship
Makes money from a friend?
Rather, lend it to your enemy.
If he fails to pay you back, you can
More decently impose the penalties.

SHYLOCK: Why, look how you storm!
I want to be friends and have your love,
Forget your shameful treatment,
And supply the money you want, and
take not a penny of interest.
I'm offering a kindness . . .

BASSANIO: Kindness indeed!

SHYLOCK: This is the kindness I'll show.
Go with me to a lawyer.
Sign an agreement, and—for fun—
If you don't pay me back as agreed,
Let the penalty be a pound of your flesh,
To be cut off and taken from
Whatever part of your body I please.

BASSANIO *(to Antonio)***:** You shall not sign
Such a contract for me! I'll manage
without.

ANTONIO: Oh, don't worry, man!
In two months—that's one month early—
I expect a return of nine times the value
Of this contract.

SHYLOCK: Oh, Father Abraham!
These Christians! Their own tough
bargains
Make them distrust everyone. Tell me this,
If he fails to pay, what would I gain by
The contract? A pound of flesh taken
From a man is not as valuable
As the flesh of sheep, beef, or goats.
I offer this friendship only to buy his
good will.
If he takes it, fine. If not, goodbye.
But don't put me in the wrong for this.

ANTONIO: Yes, Shylock. I'll sign the contract.

SHYLOCK: Then meet me at the lawyer's.
Now let me go inside and put the
money together.
I'll join you soon.

(Shylock enters his house.)

BASSANIO: I don't trust fair terms
From a villain's mind.

ANTONIO: Come, there's no cause for dismay.
My ships are due a month before the day.

(They leave together.)

ACT 2

| Scene 1 |

*Portia's house in Belmont. The **Prince of Morocco** enters, along with his **attendants**. **Portia, Nerissa**, and their **servants** await the visitors.*

MOROCCO: Do not dislike me for my color.
My dark skin is the uniform of those who
Live under the burning coppery sun.
Bring me the handsomest man of the north
Where the sun is barely hot enough
To thaw the icicles. Then let both of us
Cut our skin for your love, to prove
Whose blood is reddest, his or mine.
I tell you, lady, this face of mine
Has scared the bravest of men. But I swear
That the loveliest women of our climate
Have loved it, too.
I would not change my color
Except to win your thoughts, gentle queen.

PORTIA: In terms of choice, I am not led
By looks alone. Besides, my father's will
Does not permit me to choose my destiny.
If my father had not set up these terms,
You, famed prince, would have stood

As good a chance as any I have seen
So far of gaining my love.

MOROCCO: I thank you for that.
Therefore, please lead me to the caskets so
I can try my fortune. To win your love,
I would outstare the sternest eyes,
Pluck the baby cubs from the mother bear,
And even mock the roaring lion. But alas,
if two champions roll the dice to decide
Who is the greater man, luck may give
The weaker man the higher score. And so,
Blind fortune might cause me to lose what
A lesser man may gain, and die with grief.

PORTIA: You must take your chance.
You must either not make a choice at all,
Or swear before you choose, that if you
Make the wrong choice, never to
Propose marriage to a woman afterwards.
Therefore, think carefully.

MOROCCO: I agree to the conditions.
I'll take my chances.

PORTIA: First you must go to the temple
To swear your oath. After dinner,
You shall have your chance.

MOROCCO: Good luck to me, then!
I'll be either the most blessed or cursed
among men.

*(**All** exit.)*

| Scene 2 |

*The street in front of Shylock's house. Shylock's servant **Lancelot Gobbo** enters. He bumps into **Old Gobbo**, his father, who is nearly blind and carrying a basket.*

OLD GOBBO: Young master, please help. Which is the way to Master Jew's?

LANCELOT *(aside)*: Oh, heavens! This is my own true father! Being almost blind, he doesn't recognize me. I'll tease him a bit.
(to Old Gobbo): Turn right at the next turning, but left at the next turning of all. At the very next turning, don't turn at all, but turn down indirectly to the Jew's house!

OLD GOBBO: By all the saints, that will be hard to do. Can you tell me if Lancelot is still living with him or not?

LANCELOT *(deciding to reveal himself)*: Don't you recognize me, Father?

OLD GOBBO: Alas, I'm almost blind. I do not.

LANCELOT: Even if you had your sight, you might not know me. It is a wise father that knows his own child. Well, old man, I will tell you news of your son.
I am Lancelot, your boy that was,
Your son that is, your child that shall be.

OLD GOBBO: I can't believe you are my son!

25

LANCELOT: I don't know how to answer that. But I am Lancelot, and I am sure Margery, your wife, is my mother.

OLD GOBBO: Her name is Margery, indeed. So if you are Lancelot, I'll swear you are my own flesh and blood. Lord, how you've changed! How do you and your master get along? I have brought him a present.

LANCELOT: I've made up my mind to run away. Give him a present? Give him a *noose!* He starves me. My ribs feel like fingers. *(He guides Old Gobbo's hand to his ribs.)* Father, I am glad you've come. Give the present to a certain Master Bassanio. He really does provide smart uniforms! Either I'll serve him or keep running. Look! Here he comes. Go to him, Father. If I serve the Jew any longer, despise me!

*(**Bassanio** enters with **Leonardo** and **others**.)*

BASSANIO *(to a servant)*: Yes, but be quick about it. I want supper ready by five. Deliver these letters. Order new uniforms for the servants. Then ask Gratiano to come to my house.

*(**Servant** exits.)*

LANCELOT: Go to him, Father!

OLD GOBBO *(bowing)*: Your worship!

BASSANIO: May I help you?

OLD GOBBO: Here's my son, a poor boy—

LANCELOT *(coming forward)*: Not a poor
boy, sir, but the rich Jew's servant
who would like, as my father will
tell you—

(He hides behind his father.)

OLD GOBBO: He wishes, sir, to serve—

LANCELOT *(coming forward again)*: Well, the
short and the long of it is that I serve
the Jew, but I wish to serve you instead.

BASSANIO: I know you well. The job is yours.
Say goodbye to your old master,
And go find my house.

LANCELOT: Thank you, sir! Come on, Father.
I'll soon say farewell to the Jew.

*(**Lancelot** and his **father** exit. **Gratiano** enters, coming
up to Bassanio.)*

GRATIANO: Bassanio!

BASSANIO: Gratiano!

GRATIANO: I've a favor to ask.

BASSANIO: Granted.

GRATIANO: I must go with you to Belmont.

BASSANIO: Well then, do so. But listen—
Sometimes you are too wild, too rude,
    and too bold.
These features suit you well enough
And do not seem like faults to us.
But among strangers, they seem too much.
Please try to tone down your behavior.
Your high spirits might make me
Misunderstood in Belmont
And lose me my hopes.

GRATIANO: Bassanio, listen to me.
If I do not dress soberly, talk with respect,
And swear only now and then, like a man
    aiming to please his grandmother—
Never trust me again!

BASSANIO: Very well, we'll see how you act.

GRATIANO: But do not count tonight!
Don't judge me by what we do tonight.

BASSANIO: No, that would be a pity.
I'd rather you were at your funniest,
For our friends want to have a merry time.
But goodbye for now. I have things to do.

GRATIANO: And I must join Lorenzo now.
We will see you at dinner!

*(**They** go their separate ways.)*

| Scene 3 |

Shylock's front door. ***Jessica*** *and* ***Lancelot*** *come out.*

JESSICA: I'm sorry you are leaving my father.
But goodbye—here's a ducat for you. And,
Lancelot, please secretly give this letter
To your new master's guest, Lorenzo.

LANCELOT: Goodbye. Let my tears speak for me,
Even though such foolish tears aren't manly.
Goodbye, sweet Jessica!

JESSICA: Farewell, good Lancelot!

*(**Lancelot** exits, drying his tears.)*

Alas, what a sin it is for me to be ashamed
To be my father's child! I am his daughter,
But I am not like him.
Oh, Lorenzo, if you keep your promise,
There will be an end to this strife,
I'll become a Christian, and your
loving wife.

*(**She** goes indoors.)*

| Scene 4 |

Another street in Venice. ***Gratiano, Lorenzo, Salerio,***
and ***Solanio*** *enter, discussing preparations for their
fancy-dress party.*

LORENZO: So we will leave at suppertime,
Change our clothes at my lodging,
And be back within the hour.

GRATIANO: But we have not prepared well.

SALERIO: We haven't hired torchbearers.

SOLANIO: It's stupid unless organized well.
I don't think we should do it.

LORENZO: It's only 4:00. We have two hours
To get everything ready.

(Lancelot enters.)

Friend Lancelot, what's the news?

LANCELOT *(producing a letter)***:** Open this, and
you'll know.

GRATIANO: A love letter, I see!

LANCELOT: Excuse me, sir.

(He starts to leave.)

LORENZO: Where are you going?

LANCELOT: Well, sir, to invite my old master,
the Jew, to dine tonight with my new
master, the Christian.

LORENZO: Hold on. Take this.
(He gives him a tip.) Tell dear Jessica
I will not fail her. Tell her privately.

(Lancelot leaves.)

Go, gentlemen. Get ready for tonight.

SALERIO: Right. I'll get started on it.

SOLANIO: So will I.

LORENZO: Meet me and Gratiano
At Gratiano's place in about an hour.

SALERIO: Good idea.

(Salerio and Solanio leave.)

GRATIANO: Was that letter from fair Jessica?

LORENZO: I'd better tell you all. She told me
The way to take her from her father's
house,
What gold and jewels she will bring,
And how she will dress as a page.
If ever her father enters heaven,
It will be because of his gentle daughter.
May misfortune never cross her path.
Come with me. Read this as you go along.
Fair Jessica will be my torchbearer!

(They walk off briskly.)

| Scene 5 |

Shylock enters with Lancelot.

SHYLOCK: Well, you'll see! Your eyes
Will judge the difference between
Old Shylock and Bassanio.
(calling out) Jessica!

(to Lancelot): You won't stuff yourself as
You have with me. *(calling again)* Jessica!
(to Lancelot): Or sleep and snore,
And wear out your clothes. *(calling louder)*
What, Jessica, I say!

*(**Jessica** enters.)*

JESSICA: Did you call? What is your wish?

SHYLOCK: I'm invited out to dinner, Jessica.
Here are my keys. But why should I go?
I'm not invited out of love. They flatter me.
But still, I'll go in hate, to eat the food of
The wasteful Christian. Jessica, my girl,
Look after my house. I don't want to go.
Something doesn't feel quite right.

LANCELOT: I beg you, sir, *go!* My young master
expects the displeasure of your company.

SHYLOCK: As I do his.

LANCELOT: And they have planned something.
I won't say exactly that you'll see a
masque. But *(winking)* if you *do* see one
of those dramas, don't be surprised.

SHYLOCK: What, will there be a masque?
Listen, Jessica. Lock my doors. When
You hear the drum and the vile squealing
Of the fife player, don't look out
Into the street to see Christian fools
In painted masks. Plug my house's ears—

Don't let the sound of shallow foolishness
Enter my sober home.
I swear I have no wish to dine out
   tonight,
But I will go.
(to Lancelot): Go ahead, you. Say I'll come.

LANCELOT: I'll go ahead, sir.
(aside to Jessica): Miss, look out the window
   because *(reciting)*
   A certain Christian will come by,
   Worth the sight of a Jewess's eye.

(He leaves, whistling.)

SHYLOCK: What did that fool Gentile say?

JESSICA: He said, "Farewell, miss." No more.

SHYLOCK: The fool is kind enough,
   But a huge eater, a snail-slow worker,
   And he sleeps more by day than a wildcat.
   I'll have no lazy ones in my house,
   So I let him go—to someone he can help
      waste borrowed money.
   Jessica, go in. I may return immediately.
   Do as I say. Shut the doors behind you.

(Shylock leaves.)

JESSICA: Farewell. If my luck is not crossed,
   I've a father and you've a daughter lost.

(Jessica goes inside.)

| Scene 6 |

A street in Venice. **Gratiano** *and* **Salerio** *enter, wearing masks.*

GRATIANO: This is the balcony under which Lorenzo asked us to wait.

SALERIO: He's late.

GRATIANO: It is strange that he's not here. Lovers are usually early.

SALERIO: Look! Here he comes now.

(Lorenzo enters.)

LORENZO: Good friends, forgive my lateness. It was business, not myself, that caused it. Come. This is where my Jewish father lives. *(He calls out.)* Hello! Anybody home?

(A window opens, and **Jessica** *appears, dressed as a boy.)*

JESSICA: Who's that? Although I think I know your voice, say who you are!

LORENZO: Lorenzo, and your love!

JESSICA: Lorenzo certainly, and my love For sure! Here, catch this chest. It's worth the trouble.

(She throws it down.)

I'm glad it is night. Don't look at me,
For I am ashamed to show my clothes.
But love is blind, and lovers cannot see
Their own foolishness. If they could,
Cupid himself would blush
To see me changed into a boy.

LORENZO: Come down.
You must be my torchbearer.

JESSICA: Must I hold a candle to my shame?
Indeed, it shines out quite enough
   as it is.
Love thrives in modesty,
And I should be concealed.

LORENZO: And so you are, my sweet.
Even in the lovely disguise of a boy.
But come at once. It's getting late,
And we are expected at Bassanio's
   party.

(She closes the window.)

*(to Gratiano)***:** By heaven, I love her dearly!
If I'm any judge, she's wise, and
If my eyes tell the truth, she's beautiful!
That she is faithful, she has just proved.
Therefore her image—wise, beautiful,
   and faithful
Resides in my constant soul.

*(**Jessica** comes out of the house.)*

You are here, then. Come on, gentlemen!
Our friends are waiting for us at the party.

(They set off for the party.)

| Scene 7 |

*The hall of Portia's house in Belmont. **Portia** enters, with the **Prince of Morocco** and their **servants** and **attendants**.*

PORTIA *(to servant)*: Go, open the curtains.
Show the noble prince the three caskets.

(The curtains are drawn back, revealing three caskets displayed on a table.)

(to the prince): Now make your choice.

MOROCCO: The first, gold, bears the words:
"*Who chooses me*
Shall gain what many men desire."
The second, silver, carries this promise:
"*Who chooses me*
Shall get as much as he deserves."
The third, of dull lead, bluntly warns:
"*Who chooses me*
Must give and gamble all he has."
How shall I know if my choice is right?

PORTIA: One of these contains my picture,
Prince. If you choose that, you will be
my husband.

MOROCCO: May some god guide me!
Let me see. What does this lead casket say?
". . . must give and gamble all he has."
Must give? For what? For lead?
Risk all for lead? This casket looks
Dangerous. I'll not give or risk all for lead.
What about the silver one?
". . . shall get as much as he deserves."
Pause there, Morocco. Weigh your value.
I deserve enough, but "enough"
Might not stretch as far as to the lady.
And yet I should not underestimate myself.
As much as I deserve— Why, that's the lady!
What if I went no further, but chose here?
Let's see once more the saying on the gold.
". . . shall gain what many men desire."
That's the lady—all the world desires her.
One of the three holds her heavenly
  picture.
Is it likely that lead contains her?
I don't think so. Nor do I think she's in
The silver, which is worth less than gold.
Give me the key. I choose the gold one,
And take my chance!

PORTIA *(handing him the key)***:** Take it, Prince.
If my picture is inside, then I am yours.

(He opens the golden casket.)

MOROCCO: Oh, no! What have we here?
A rotting skull, with a rolled-up
    manuscript stuffed
In its empty eye socket. I'll read it.
"All that glitters is not gold;
Often you have heard that told.
Many a man his life has sold,
Just my outside to behold.
Golden tombs do worms enfold.
Had you been as wise as bold,
Young in limbs, in wisdom old,
Your answer would not be enscrolled—
Fare you well. Your suit is cold.
Cold indeed, and labor lost.

So farewell heat, and welcome frost."
Portia, goodbye! I have too sad a heart
For a long farewell. Thus losers depart.

*(Bowing, **he** leaves with his **attendants**.)*

PORTIA *(to Nerissa)***:** Good riddance!
*(to servant)***:** Close the curtains. Go.
May all with his vanity leave me so.

*(**They** exit.)*

| Scene 8 |

*A street in Venice. **Salerio** and **Solanio** enter.*

SALERIO: Why, man, I saw Bassanio set sail.
Gratiano has gone along with him.
I am sure Lorenzo is not on board.

SOLANIO: The villainous Jew with his outcries
Roused the duke, who went with him
To search Bassanio's ship.

SALERIO: He was too late. The ship was gone.
But someone said that Lorenzo and Jessica
Were seen together in a gondola.
Besides, Antonio told the duke that
They were not with Bassanio in his ship.

SOLANIO: I never heard such an outcry
As the Jew did utter in the streets.
"My daughter! My ducats! My daughter!

Fled with a Christian! Justice! The law!
My ducats, and my daughter! A sealed bag!
Two bags of golden ducats
Stolen from me by my daughter!
And jewels—two precious stones—
Stolen by my daughter! Find the girl!
She has the stones and the money!"

SALERIO *(laughing)***:** All the boys in Venice
Follow him, crying, "His stones!
His daughter! His money!"

SOLANIO *(serious now)***:** Antonio had better
Pay his loan on time, or he will pay for this.

SALERIO: You're right.
I chatted with a Frenchman yesterday,
Who said that a rich Venetian ship had
Foundered in the English Channel.
I thought about Antonio when he told me,
And wished in silence that it wasn't his.

SOLANIO: You'd better tell Antonio about it.
But do it gently. It may grieve him.

SALERIO: There's no kinder man on earth!
I saw Bassanio and Antonio part.
Bassanio said he'd return quickly.
Antonio said, "Do not hurry for my sake.
Stay as long as you must. As for the
Jew's contract, don't let it affect
Your love plans. Be merry, and focus
On courtship and such shows of love

That seem proper there." At this point,
His eyes filled with tears. Turning his face,
He put his hand out behind him, and with
Great affection, he shook Bassanio's hand.
And so they parted.

SOLANIO: I think he means the world to him.
Let's go find him and cheer him up.

SALERIO: Let's do that.

*(**They** leave.)*

| Scene 9 |

*Portia's house at Belmont. The casket room. **Nerissa**
and a **servant** enter.*

NERISSA: Quick! Please draw the curtain!
The Prince of Aragon has taken his oath,
And he's coming to make his choice now.

*(The servant closes the curtains. **Portia**, the **Prince of
Aragon**, and their **attendants** enter.)*

PORTIA: There are the caskets, noble Prince.
If you choose the one with my picture in it,
We shall be married right away.
But if you fail, you must leave
    immediately.

ARAGON: I know the risk. May fortune now
Grant me my heart's hope!

Gold, silver, and base lead.
"Who chooses me
Must give and gamble all he has."
(addressing the lead casket): You must
Look fairer before I'd give and gamble all.
What does the golden chest say?
"Who chooses me
Shall gain what many men desire."
I will not choose what many men desire,
Because I am not like the common masses.
Well then, to you, silver treasure house!
Tell me once more what you say.
"Who chooses me
Shall get as much as he deserves."
That is my choice. Give me the key for this.

(He opens the silver casket.)

What's here? The portrait of a fool,
Offering me a note. I will read it.
(looking at the picture) How unlike you
Are to Portia! How unlike my hopes and
My deservings! Did I deserve no more
Than a clown's head?

(opening the document and reading)

"Some there are that shadows kiss,
Some have but a shadow's bliss.
There are fools alive, I say,
Who are silvered over in this way.
It matters not which wife you wed,

I will always be your head.
So be off, for you are sped."
(to Portia) A greater fool I shall appear
The longer that I linger here.
With one fool's head I came to woo,
But I go away with two.
Sweet, farewell, my word I'll keep,
To bear with patience my sorrows deep.

(He leaves with his attendants.)

PORTIA *(relieved)***:** Another moth burned
By the candle! Oh, these pompous fools!
Thinking they can so wisely choose,
They're so surprised when they lose.

NERISSA: The old words said it straight—
To hang or to marry is a matter of fate.

PORTIA: Come, draw the curtain, Nerissa.

(She does so. A servant enters.)

SERVANT: Madam, a young Venetian is here.
He has brought gifts of great value.
Until now I have not seen so promising
An ambassador of love.

PORTIA: Come, Nerissa, for I long to see this
Messenger of Cupid who seems so gentle.

NERISSA: May it be Bassanio, Lord willing!

(All exit.)

ACT 3

| Scene 1 |

The street in front of Shylock's house in Venice.
Solanio *meets **Salerio**, who has just come from the*
Rialto, the business center.

SOLANIO: What's the news on the Rialto?

SALERIO: There's a story going around
That one of Antonio's ships has been
Wrecked in the English Channel.

SOLANIO: What's that? He's lost a ship?

SALERIO: I hope it's the end of his losses.

SOLANIO: Let me say "Amen" at once,
In case the devil thwarts my prayer,
For here he comes in the form of a Jew.

(*Shylock* comes out of his house.)

Well now, Shylock! What's the news?

SHYLOCK *(angrily)*: You knew—none so well
as you—of my daughter's flight.

SALERIO: Of course! I even knew the tailor
Who made the wings for her!

SOLANIO: Shylock knew the bird was ready
To fly—and that it is natural
For young birds to leave their mothers.

SHYLOCK: She is damned for it!

SALERIO: Oh, yes, if the devil is her judge.

SHYLOCK: My own flesh and blood to rebel!

SOLANIO *(pretending to misunderstand)*: Fancy
    that, old skin and bones.
    What, at your age?

SHYLOCK: I mean my daughter, who is my
    flesh and blood.

SALERIO: Your flesh and hers are
    More different than jet black and ivory.
    Your bloods are more different
    Than red wine and white.
    But tell us now—have you heard whether
    Antonio has had any loss at sea?

SHYLOCK: There I made another bad deal.
    A bankrupt. A prodigal. He hardly dares to
    Show his face on the Rialto. A beggar now,
    Who used to come so smugly to town.
    He'd better honor his bond!

SALERIO: Well, I'm sure if he can't,
    You won't take his flesh.
    After all, what is it good for?

SHYLOCK: To bait fish with! If it will feed
    Nothing else, it will feed my revenge.
    He has disgraced me, hindered me,
    Laughed at my losses, mocked my gains.
    He has scorned my nationality,
    Thwarted my deals, cooled my friends,

Angered my enemies. And why?
  I am a Jew. But hasn't a Jew got eyes?
Doesn't a Jew have hands, organs, limbs,
Senses, affections, passions?
Isn't he fed with the same food,
Hurt by the same weapons,
Subject to the same diseases,
Healed by the same means,
Warmed and cooled by the
Same winter and summer, as a Christian is?
  If you prick us, do we not bleed?
If you tickle us, do we not laugh?
If you poison us, do we not die?
And if you wrong us,
Shall we not seek revenge?
If we are like you in everything else,
We will be like you in that.
  If a Jew wrongs a Christian,
What is his natural response? Revenge.
If a Christian wrongs a Jew, what should
His penalty be—by Christian example?
Why, revenge!
The villainy you teach me, I will carry out.
And I'll go one better if I get the chance!

*(A **servant** stops Solanio and Salerio.)*

SERVANT: Sirs, my master Antonio is at home.
  He would like to speak to you both.

SALERIO: We've been looking for him.

*(**Solanio**, **Salerio**, and the **servant** leave. **Tubal** comes toward Shylock's house.)*

SHYLOCK: Greetings, Tubal. What news
From Genoa? Did you find my daughter?

TUBAL: I heard her spoken of,
But I could not find her.

SHYLOCK: No news of them? All right.
And I don't know what the search
Has cost so far. Loss upon loss!
The thief gone with so much, and
So much more spent to find the thief,
yet no satisfaction! No revenge!
No bad luck anywhere
Except what falls on my shoulders.
No sighs but my sighs. No tears but mine!

(He cries.)

TUBAL: Yes, other men have bad luck, too.
Antonio, as I heard in Genoa . . .

SHYLOCK *(recovering quickly)***:** What, what?
Bad luck? Bad luck, you say?

TUBAL: He's lost a ship coming from Tripoli.

SHYLOCK: I thank God! Is it true?

TUBAL: I spoke to some of the sailors
Who escaped from the wreck.

SHYLOCK: Thank you, Tubal. Good news!
Ha, ha! You heard this in Genoa?

TUBAL *(changing the subject)*: I also heard
That your daughter spent eighty ducats
in one night.

SHYLOCK: You stick a dagger in me!
I shall never see my gold again.
Eighty ducats at a sitting! Eighty ducats!

TUBAL *(switching back again)*: Several of
Antonio's creditors came to me in Venice.
They swear he'll soon be bankrupt.

SHYLOCK: I'm glad of it. I'll plague him.
I'll torture him. I'm glad of it!

TUBAL *(getting back to Jessica)*: One of them
Showed me a ring that your daughter
Had traded with him for a monkey.

SHYLOCK: You torture me, Tubal!
Leah gave me that ring before we married.
I would not have traded it
For a wilderness of monkeys.

TUBAL *(trying to ease Shylock's pain)*: But Antonio
is certainly ruined.

SHYLOCK: Yes, that's true. Go, find a sheriff.
I'll give Antonio two weeks' notice.
If he can't pay, I'll have his heart!
Once he's out of Venice, I can do business
My own way. Go, Tubal—and meet me
At our synagogue.

(They leave, going separate ways.)

| Scene 2 |

The hall of Portia's house at Belmont. The curtains are drawn back, revealing the caskets. **Bassanio** *is ready to make his choice.*

PORTIA: Wait a little, please. Pause a day
Or two before you take the gamble. If you
Choose wrong, I'll lose your company.
Therefore, wait a while. Something tells me
   that I don't want to lose you.
You know yourself that hatred does not
Give such advice. But in case you do not
Understand me well—for maidens can only
Think their thoughts, not speak them—
I'd like to keep you here a month or two
   before you make your choice.
I could teach you how to choose right,
But I'm under oath not to. If you don't win,
I'll never be another's. If you should fail,
You'll make me wish something sinful—
That I had broken my oath and advised you.
   Shame on your eyes!
They've looked at me, dividing me in two.
Half of me is yours. The other half, too.
I ought to say "my own," but what is mine
Is yours, so all of me is yours.
I talk too much, but it's to slow down time,
Draw it out, and stretch out its length
To delay the making of your choice.

BASSANIO: Let me choose.
As I am, I'm living on the rack of torment.

PORTIA: On the rack, Bassanio! Confess then
What treason is mingled with your love!

BASSANIO: Only the ugly treason of mistrust,
Which makes me fear enjoying my love.
Snow and fire might just as well be
   friends,
As treason and my love.

PORTIA: Yes, but I'm afraid the rack makes
You say anything, like any tortured man.

BASSANIO: Promise me life,
And I'll confess the truth!

PORTIA: Well then, confess and live.

BASSANIO: "Confess and love" would be my
Full confession. Oh, happy torment,
When my torturer gives me the answers
To set me free. But let me
Test my fortune with the caskets.

PORTIA: Go then! I am locked in one of them.
If you really love me, you will find me.
(to the onlookers): Nerissa and the rest,
Stand aside. Let music play as he chooses.
That way, if he loses, he can leave
Like a dying swan, fading in music.

(One servant stays while the others go to the musicians' gallery.)

To extend the comparison, my tears will be
The stream and watery deathbed for him.
(more cheerfully) He may win.
What of music then? Oh, then, music
    would be like the dawn chorus that
Creeps into the dreaming bridegroom's ear,
Calling him to his wedding. There he goes,
(to Bassanio): Go, love! If you win, I live!

(Music plays while Bassanio thinks.)

BASSANIO: The world is fooled by ornament.
In law, any plea, no matter how corrupt,
Can hide its evil behind a saintly voice.
In religion, any heresy can be blessed by
Some learned man who uses the Scriptures
    in support of its grossness.
How many cowards, with hearts as false
As stairs made from sand, sport beards
Like brave Hercules and warlike Mars?
They only wear those beards to seem tough.
    Look on beauty. You'll see that it's often
Purchased by the ounce.
Cosmetics work miracles. Those with the
Lightest morals use them most heavily.
Ornament is the rocky shore of a most
Dangerous sea, the beautiful scarf veiling
An uncertain beauty. Therefore, gaudy gold,
    I want none of you. Nor of you, silver,
The stuff of common coins. But you,

51

Worthless lead, which threatens
Rather than promises, your paleness
Moves me more than eloquence.
I choose you. May joy be the result!

(The servant hands him the key.)

PORTIA *(aside)***:** How fast all other passions
Disappear—doubt, despair, fear,
And green-eyed jealousy! Oh, love,
Be moderate, control your ecstasy,
Restrain your joy! Don't get too excited—
I feel your blessing too much. Make it less,
In case it overwhelms me!

BASSANIO *(opening the casket)***:** What's this?
Fair Portia's portrait! *(admiring it)* Divine!
Do these eyes move? Or do they merely
Reflect the motion of mine? Here are lips
Parted with sugar breath! Here in her hair
    the painter has, like a spider,
Woven a golden net to entrap men's hearts,
Faster than gnats in cobwebs. But her eyes!
How could he see to do them? After he
Painted one, it would have had the power to
Blind him, denying itself a companion.
    But look! Just as my praises undervalue
The portrait, so does this portrait
Fall short of the reality. Here's the scroll,
On which my fortune is summarized:

(He reads the scroll.)

"You who choose not by the view
Take fair chance, and choose quite true.
Since this fortune falls to you,
Be content, seek nothing new.
If you be well-pleased with this
And see your fortune as your bliss,
Turn to where your lady is,
And claim her with a loving kiss."
A kindly scroll! *(He turns to Portia.)*
I come to you with a permit, by your leave,
(offering the scroll as a permit for a kiss)
A kiss to give and to receive.
But only if this is agreeable to you.
I wait to hear your answer true.

PORTIA: You see me, Lord Bassanio, as I am.
For myself, I would not seek improvement.
But for you, I wish I were 60 times better,
A thousand times more beautiful,
Ten thousand times richer.
  I'm really very little—at best
An uneducated and inexperienced girl.
Happily, not too old to learn.
Happier still, not too stupid to learn.
Happiest of all—I surrender myself to you,
My lord, governor, and king.

(They kiss, meeting the terms of the scroll.)
Myself, and what is mine, are now yours.
Until now I was the lord of this fine house,

Master of my servants, queen over myself.
Now, this house, these servants, and
  myself
Are yours. I give them with this ring.

(She puts a ring on Bassanio's finger.)

If you part with it, lose it, or give it away,
That will mean the end of your love
And be my reason to denounce you.

BASSANIO: Madam, I don't know what to say!
Only the blood in my veins speaks to you.
I am like a crowd of people overwhelmed
  by the fine speech of a beloved prince.
Every atom of my being is shouting with
Wild cheers of joy. When this ring
Parts from this finger, life parts from me.
Then you could confidently say,
"This means that Bassanio is dead."

*(**Nerissa** and **Gratiano** join them.)*

NERISSA: Good joy, my lord and lady!

GRATIANO: Lord Bassiano and gentle lady,
I wish you great joy. And when the time
Comes for your wedding, I beg you
That at that time I can be married, too!

BASSANIO: Of course—if you can find a wife.

GRATIANO: Thanking your lordship,
You have found me one.

(He takes Nerissa's hand.)

My eyes, my lord, are just as swift as yours.
You saw the mistress—I spotted the maid.
You loved, I loved.
Your fortune depended on the caskets
   there,
And so did mine, as it happened.
I wooed until I sweated, and swore
Oaths of love until my mouth ran dry.
At last I got a promise of her hand
From this fair lady here,
On condition that you won her mistress.

PORTIA: Is this true, Nerissa?

NERISSA: Madam, it is, if you are pleased.

BASSANIO: Do you mean it, Gratiano?

GRATIANO: Yes indeed, my lord.

BASSANIO: Our wedding feast will be
Most honored by your marriage.

GRATIANO *(to Nerissa)***:** We'll bet them
A thousand ducats that we have a son first.

NERISSA *(blushing)***:** What, betting on that?

GRATIANO *(teasing)***:** We'll never win,
If we don't get started soon!

*(**Lorenzo** and **Jessica** enter, followed by **Salerio**, who is carrying a letter.)*

But who's this? Lorenzo and Jessica?
What—and my old Venetian friend,
   Salerio?

BASSANIO: Lorenzo and Salerio, welcome.
If one so new in my status here can do so,
I bid you welcome.
(to Portia): With your permission, sweet
Portia.

PORTIA: They are entirely welcome, my lord.

LORENZO *(to Bassanio)*: I thank your honor.
For my part, I did not plan to see you here.
But I met Salerio on the way,
And he begged me to come along.
He wouldn't take no for an answer.

SALERIO: I did, my lord, with good reason.

(He gives Bassanio the letter.)

Antonio sends his respects.

BASSANIO: Before I open his letter,
Tell me how my good friend is doing.

SALERIO: Not sick—unless it's in his mind.
Yet not well either, unless you mean
mentally.
His letter explains his situation.

(Bassanio opens the letter.)

GRATIANO *(nodding toward Jessica)*: Nerissa,
Cheer up our stranger. Bid her welcome.

(Nerissa greets Jessica, while Gratiano shakes hands with Salerio.)

Your hand, Salerio. What's new in Venice?

How is Antonio getting along?
I know he will be happy for us!

SALERIO: He'll be happy for you, I'm sure.
But things are not going so well for him.

(He takes Gratiano to one side to explain.)

PORTIA *(observing Bassanio as he reads)***:** There are
some sad contents in that letter
That rob the color from Bassanio's cheek.
Some dear friend dead? What—worse?
(She touches his arm.) With respect,
Bassanio, I am half yourself. I will freely
Share half of any trouble this letter brings
you.

BASSANIO: Sweet Portia! Here are some of the
Saddest words that ever blotted paper!
Dear lady, when I first told you of my love,
I freely confessed that all my wealth
Ran in my veins. I was a gentleman,
So I told you the truth. And yet, dear lady,
When I told you I had nothing, you will see
That I was bragging. I should have told you
That I had less than nothing. Actually,
I am indebted to a dear friend, who lent me
Money borrowed from his worst enemy.
    Here is a letter, lady.
The paper represents my friend's body,
And every word in it is a gaping wound,
Leaking his life's blood. But is it true,

Salerio, that all his investments have
  failed?
Not one success? From Tripoli, Mexico,
England? From Lisbon, Barbary, India?
Not one ship escaped the dreadful touch of
Shipwrecking rocks?

SALERIO: Not one, my lord. Besides, it seems
That even if he could pay the loan,
The Jew would not take the money.
I never knew a creature in human form
  so sharp and hungry to destroy a man.
He appeals to the duke morning and night.
He says it is unlawful to deny him justice.
The duke, the nobles, and 20 merchants
Have argued with him. But he won't
  listen.

JESSICA: When I lived with him, I heard him
Swear that he'd rather have Antonio's flesh
Than 20 times the amount he owes.
I know, my lord, that if law, authority,
And power don't stop him,
It will go hard with poor Antonio.

PORTIA: Is Antonio your dear friend?

BASSANIO: My dearest friend.
The kindest man, the best meaning
And most tireless of those
Who do good deeds. He is one with more
Roman honor in him than any man in Italy.

PORTIA: How much does he owe the Jew?

BASSANIO: On my behalf, 3,000 ducats.

PORTIA: No more? Pay him 6,000! No,
Two times that. And then three times that!
No friend of that description
Shall lose a hair through Bassanio's fault.
First go with me to church and call me wife.
Then go to Venice to your friend.
   You shall not lie by Portia's side
With a troubled spirit. Take enough gold
To pay the petty debt 20 times over.
When it is paid, bring your true friend here.
Nerissa and I will live as maids and widows
Until you come back. Away, now!
   You must leave on your wedding day.
Bid welcome to your friends. Smile!
Since you are dearly bought,
I'll love you dearly.
Let me hear your friend's letter.

BASSANIO *(reading)***:** *"Dear Bassanio, my ships
have all been wrecked. My creditors grow
cruel. My assets are very low. My bond to
the Jew is forfeit. In paying it, I cannot
possibly live. But all debts between us will
be cleared—if, at my death, I could but see
you. Even so, do as you wish. If your love
for me does not persuade you to come, don't
let this letter do so."*

PORTIA: Oh, my love! Hurry to him!

BASSANIO: Since you have given your consent,
  I'll go. But, until I return, I will
  Neither sleep nor rest!

*(**Everyone** hurries off.)*

| Scene 3 |

*Outside Shylock's house. **Shylock** stands at his door,
with **Antonio**, **Solanio**, and **Jailer**.*

SHYLOCK: Jailer, guard him well!
  Don't talk to me of mercy!
  This is the fool who lent out money
  Free of interest. Jailer, guard him.

ANTONIO: Listen a minute, good Shylock—

SHYLOCK: I will have my bond! Don't speak
  Against my bond. I've sworn an oath
  That I will have my bond. You called me
   a dog before you had a reason.
  Since I am a dog, beware my fangs!
  The duke will grant me justice. I'm amazed,
  You wicked jailer, that you are so foolish
  As to wander about with him at his request!

ANTONIO: Please, hear me speak!

SHYLOCK: *I'll have my bond.* Do not speak!
  I'll not be made into a soft and stupid fool,

Shaking my head, sighing, and giving in
To Christian pleas. Don't follow me.
Don't speak to me! I will have my bond!

*(**He** enters his house, slamming the door.)*

SOLANIO: He's the most stubborn dog
Who ever kept company with men.

ANTONIO: Leave him alone.
I'll follow him no more with useless pleas.
He wants my life. I know his reason well.
I often paid others' debts to him when
They asked me for help. So he hates me.

SOLANIO: I'm sure the duke will never
Rule in favor of the terms of this bond.

ANTONIO: The duke cannot change the law.
  If we denied the rights of strangers
  Here in Venice, it would go against
  Our ideas of justice. The city trades
  With people of all nations.
    I've lost so much weight
  Because of my griefs and losses
  That tomorrow I can hardly spare a pound
  Of flesh to my bloodthirsty creditor.
  Well, jailer, let's move on. If only
  Bassanio will come to see me pay his debt.
  Then I shall be content!

(They exit.)

| Scene 4 |

Portia's house in Belmont. **Portia, Nerissa, Lorenzo, Jessica,** *and Portia's servant* **Balthazar** *enter.*

LORENZO: Madam, you have a truly noble
  Understanding of friendship.
  If you knew the man you are honoring—
  How true a gentleman he is, how dearly
  He loves your husband—I know you
  Would be even prouder of what you did.

PORTIA: I've never regretted doing good
  And do not now. Between friends
  Who talk and spend time together,

And who love each other equally,
There must be a similarity in spirit.
This makes me think that Antonio,
  being a close friend of my husband,
Must be like him. If that is so,
How cheaply have I rescued a soulmate
From hellish cruelty. This sounds too much
Like praising myself, so that's enough!
  To change the subject, Lorenzo,
I want you to take over the management
Of my household until my husband returns.
For myself, I've made a secret vow to live
Alone in prayer and contemplation,
Except for Nerissa here,
Until our husbands return.
There is a monastery two miles away.
  We'll live there.
I hope you won't deny my request,
Which I ask out of love and pressing need.

LORENZO: Madam, with my whole heart,
  I shall obey all of your commands.

PORTIA: My servants already know my plans.
  They will accept you and Jessica
  In place of Lord Bassanio and myself.
  So farewell until we meet again!

LORENZO: Farewell to you, dear lady.

*(**Jessica** and **Lorenzo** exit.)*

PORTIA: Now, Balthazar! You've always been
Honest and true. Let me find you so now.
(handing him a letter) Take this letter,
And get to Padua as fast as you can.
Give this to my cousin, Doctor Bellario,
And he'll give you certain documents
And clothing. Bring them to the crossing
Where the public ferry trades with Venice.
Waste no time in words, but just go!
I'll be there before you.

BALTHAZAR: Madam, I'll go quickly.

(He leaves.)

PORTIA: Come on, Nerissa. I have work to do
That you do not know about. We'll see
Our husbands before they think of us.

NERISSA: Will they see us?

PORTIA: They will, Nerissa, but they'll think,
By our clothes, that we are male.
I will bet you that
When we're dressed as young men,
I will be the handsomer of the two.
I'll wear my dagger more bravely, speak in
The high-pitched voice of an adolescent,
Turn my maidenly steps into a manly
  stride,
And boast of brawls like a bragging youth.
I'll lie about how many hearts I've broken,

So that people will swear that I left school
At least twelve months ago.

NERISSA: What—are we to turn into men?

PORTIA: Dear me! What a silly question!
But come. I'll tell you my plan when we're
In my coach, which waits at the park gate.
Let's hurry. We must cover twenty miles
   today!

*(**They** rush away.)*

ACT 4

| Scene 1 |

A court of law in Venice. **Antonio** *enters between two* **guards**, *followed by* **Bassanio, Gratiano, Solanio, officers**, *and* **clerks**, *and finally,* **the duke.**

DUKE: Well, is Antonio here?

ANTONIO: Ready, your honor.

DUKE: I am sorry for you. You have come
To answer a hard-hearted adversary,
An inhuman wretch incapable of pity,
Totally empty of even a drop of mercy!

ANTONIO: I shall meet his fury
With patience. I'm ready to suffer his rage
With a quietness of spirit.

DUKE: Go, someone,
And call the Jew into the court.

SOLANIO: He is already at the door.
He's coming, my lord.

DUKE: Make way for him,
And let him stand before me.

(The crowd parts and **Shylock** *stands before the duke, bowing low.)*

Shylock, the world thinks—and so do I—

That you plan to keep up this malice only
Until the last minute. Then it's thought that
You will show mercy and remorse even
   stranger than this apparent cruelty.
And where you now demand the penalty,
   a pound of this poor merchant's flesh,
You will finally relent. Touched with
Human gentleness and love, you will even
Forgive part of the original debt. Some say
That you'll have pity because of the losses
That have recently fallen so heavily on him.
Such losses would cripple a royal merchant
And touch the hardest of hearts.

(He pauses.)

We all expect a gentle answer, Shylock.

SHYLOCK: I have told your grace my plans.
I have sworn by our holy Sabbath to have
Full payment for default on my bond.
If you deny it, let the danger fall upon
Your city's constitution and freedom.
   You'll ask me why I choose to have
A pound of dead flesh rather than to receive
Three thousand ducats. I'll not answer that!
But say it is my whim! Is it answered?
What if my house is troubled with a rat,
And I am pleased to give 10,000 ducats
To have it poisoned? Is that answer good?
I won't give any other reason, apart from
   the firm hatred that I have for Antonio,

For pursuing a losing battle with him.
Are you answered now?

BASSANIO: This is no answer, you unfeeling
man, to make excuses for your cruelty!

SHYLOCK: I am not obliged to please you
With my answers!

BASSANIO: Do all men kill the things
They do not love?

SHYLOCK: Wouldn't any man want
To kill the things he hates?

BASSANIO: Not every offense causes hate.

SHYLOCK: What—would you let a snake
Sting you twice?

ANTONIO *(to Bassanio)***:** You think you can
Reason with the Jew? You may as well
Go stand upon the beach and tell the tide
Not to reach its usual height.
Or you might as well ask the wolf why
He has made the ewe cry for its lamb.
You may as well forbid the mountain pines
To sway or to make a noise when they are
Buffeted by the winds. Anything that hard
You might as well try to do, as try to soften
that hardest thing of all—his heart.
Therefore, I beg you make no more offers,
Use no other methods. As soon as possible,
Let me know the court's decision,

And let the Jew have his will!

BASSANIO: I offer double your 3,000 ducats!

SHYLOCK: If every one of your 6,000 ducats
Were in six parts, and every part a ducat,
I would not take it. I demand my bond!

DUKE: How can you hope for mercy,
When you give none?

SHYLOCK: What judgment should I dread,
Having done no wrong? Many among you
Have slaves. You use them like your dogs
And mules—for wretched jobs, because
You bought them. Shall I say to you,
"Set them free. Marry them to your heirs.
Why should they sweat, carrying burdens?
Let their beds be as soft as yours, and
Their food as good." You would answer,
  "The slaves are ours." I say the same.
The pound of flesh which I demand of him
Is dearly bought. It is mine. I will have it.
If you deny me, I scorn your laws!
The decrees of Venice have no force.
I insist on justice. Answer! Shall I have it?

DUKE: I have the power to dismiss this court,
Unless Bellario, a learned doctor of law,
Whom I have sent for to resolve this case,
Comes here today.

SOLANIO: My lord, a messenger has just come
From Padua, with letters from the doctor.

DUKE: Bring me the letters.

BASSANIO: Cheer up, Antonio! Be brave!
The Jew shall have my flesh, blood, bones,
And all, before you shall lose
One drop of blood for me.

(Shylock takes out a knife and begins to sharpen it on the soles of his leather shoes.)

ANTONIO: I am the weakest ram in the flock,
Best suited for death. The weakest fruit
Drops first to the ground, and so let me.
You cannot be better used, Bassanio,
Than to stay alive and write my epitaph.

*(**Nerissa** enters, dressed as a judge's clerk.)*

DUKE: Did you come from Bellario?

NERISSA: Yes. He sends his greetings.

(She presents a letter, which the duke reads.)

BASSANIO *(to Shylock):* Why do you
Sharpen your knife so earnestly?

SHYLOCK: To cut out my pound of flesh.

GRATIANO: You sharpen it not on your
Shoe's sole but on your immortal soul!
No metal, not even the executioner's axe,
Is half as keen as your sharp envy.
Can no prayers touch you?

SHYLOCK: None that you have brains to make.

GRATIANO: Damn you, you stubborn dog!

Justice is to blame for letting you live.
I almost doubt my faith and share the theory
That the souls of animals can enter men.
Your spirit comes from a wolf whose soul,
When he was hanged for killing humans,
Fled into the womb of your unholy mother
And settled into you! Your desires
Are wolfish, bloody, mean, and hungry!

SHYLOCK: Until you can remove the seal from
My bond, you merely damage your lungs
To speak so loud. I'm here for justice.

DUKE: This letter from Bellario commends
A young and learned doctor of law
To our court. Where is he?

NERISSA: He is waiting nearby to hear
Your answer. Will you admit him?

DUKE: With all my heart. Three or four of you,
Go and escort him to this place.

(Attendants leave.)

Now, the court shall hear Bellario's letter.

(He reads.)

*"Your grace, when your letter arrived, I was
very sick. But when your messenger came,
a young doctor of law from Rome was
visiting me. I told him of the lawsuit
between Shylock and Antonio. We
consulted many books together. I have*

asked him to come to you in my place.
I beg you, do not underestimate him
because of his lack of years. I never knew
so young a body with so old a head.
I trust you will accept him. His
performance will speak for itself."

(He looks up.)

You hear what Bellario has written.

*(**Portia** enters, dressed as a judge, carrying a lawbook.)*

And here, I take it, is the doctor himself.
(He greets her.) Give me your hand.
(They shake.) You came from old Bellario?

PORTIA: I did, my lord.

DUKE: You are welcome. Take your place.

(A court usher guides Portia to a desk near the duke.)

Are you familiar with the case
Before the court?

PORTIA: Yes, I am.
Which is the merchant, and which the Jew?

DUKE: Antonio and Shylock, stand up.

PORTIA: Is your name Shylock?

SHYLOCK: Shylock is my name.

PORTIA: Your case is unusual.
But it is sound enough that Venetian laws
Cannot stop you from proceeding.
(to Antonio): You stand in some danger

From him, do you not?

ANTONIO: Yes, so he says.

PORTIA: Do you admit to the bond?

ANTONIO: I do.

PORTIA: Then the Jew must be merciful.

SHYLOCK: And what forces me to be? Tell me!

PORTIA: The quality of mercy is not strained.
It drops like a gentle rain from heaven
Upon the place beneath. It is twice blessed.
It blesses him that gives, and him that takes.
It is mightiest in the mightiest. It is more
    becoming to the king than his crown.
His scepter shows his earthly power,
The symbol of his awe and majesty,
The reason kings are held in fear and dread.
    But mercy is above this sceptered rule.
It is enthroned in the hearts of kings.
It is a quality of God himself.
Earthly power is nearest to God's
When mercy balances justice. So, Jew—
Though you claim justice, consider this:
None of us could expect salvation if justice
Alone won out. We pray for mercy,
And that same prayer teaches us all to do
The deeds of mercy. I have said all this
    to soften the justice of your pleas.
If you insist on it, this strict court of Venice

Has no choice but to pronounce sentence
Against the merchant there.

SHYLOCK: I'll answer for my own sins!
I want the law to enforce my bond!

PORTIA: Is he not able to pay the money?

BASSANIO: Yes, I offer it to him now in court.
It is twice the sum. If that is not enough,
I will pay ten times the amount,
On forfeit of my hands, my head, my heart!
If this is not enough, malice hides the truth.

(He kneels before Portia as if in prayer.)

I beg you: Twist the law your way.
To do a great right, do a little wrong, and

74

Stop this cruel devil from having his will!

PORTIA: That cannot be. No power in Venice
Can change a standing law. It would create
A precedent, and cause many errors
By the same example. It cannot be.

SHYLOCK: Oh, wise young judge, I honor you!

(He kisses the hem of her robe.)

PORTIA: Allow me to read the bond.

SHYLOCK *(handing it over)*: Here it is,
Most reverend doctor. Here it is!

PORTIA *(accepting the document without reading it)*:
Shylock, three times
Your money has been offered to you.

SHYLOCK: My oath! My oath!
I have vowed an oath to heaven!
Shall my soul be guilty of perjury?
No—not even for all of Venice!

PORTIA *(reading the bond)*: Why, this bond
Is forfeit. By this, the Jew may lawfully
Claim a pound of flesh, to be cut off by him
Nearest to the merchant's heart.
(to Shylock): Be merciful. Take three times
The money. Tell me to tear up the bond.

SHYLOCK: When it is paid according to the
Agreement. You appear to be a good judge.
You know the law. In the name of
The law, I demand judgment.

ANTONIO: I strongly beg the court
To give the judgment.

PORTIA *(to Antonio)*: Well, then, here it is:
You must prepare your breast for his knife.

SHYLOCK: Noble judge! Excellent young man!

PORTIA: The purpose of the law is to support
The penalty, which *(indicating the bond)*
Here seems due, according to the bond.

SHYLOCK: That's very true. Oh, wise judge!

PORTIA *(to Antonio)*: So, lay bare your breast.

SHYLOCK: Yes, his chest. So says the bond,
"Nearest his heart." The very words.

PORTIA: That's so. Are there scales here,
To weigh the flesh?

SHYLOCK: I have them ready.

(He opens his cloak to show them.)

PORTIA: Order a doctor to stand by, Shylock,
To stop his wounds
So he won't bleed to death.

SHYLOCK: Does it say that in the bond?

(He takes up the document and reads it.)

PORTIA: It is not spelled out, but what of that?
You'd do that much out of charity.

SHYLOCK: I can't find it. It's not in the bond.

(He hands back the document.)

PORTIA: Merchant, have you anything to say?

ANTONIO: Very little. I am well-prepared.
Give me your hand, Bassanio. Farewell.
  Don't grieve about this.
In my case, Fortune is kinder than usual.
Often she lets the wretched man outlive
His wealth, to endure with sunken eyes
And wrinkled brow an old age of poverty.
She has spared me that lingering misery.
Remember me to your honorable wife.
  Tell her how Antonio came to die,
And say how I loved you.
Speak well of me in death.
When the tale is told, ask her to judge
Whether or not Bassanio was loved.
  Only regret that you lose your friend
Who has no regret about paying your
  debt.
If the Jew cuts deep enough,
I'll pay it instantly, with all my heart!

BASSANIO: Antonio, I am married to a wife
Who is as dear to me as life itself.
But life itself, my wife, and all the world
Are not more precious to me than your life.
I would lose all—yes, sacrifice them all—
To save you!

PORTIA: Your wife would not thank you for
That, if she heard you make such an offer.

GRATIANO: I have a wife whom I swear I love.
I wish she were in heaven, so she could
Beg some power to change this Jew!

NERISSA: It's well you say it behind her back.
That wish would make an unhappy house.

SHYLOCK *(aside)*: These Christian husbands!
I have a daughter. I'd rather she married
Anyone else besides a Christian!
(aloud) We're wasting time. I beg you,
Proceed to sentence.

PORTIA: A pound of that merchant's flesh
Is yours. The court awards it,
And the law permits it.

SHYLOCK: Most rightful judge!

PORTIA: You must cut it from his breast.
The law allows it, and the court awards it.

SHYLOCK: Most learned judge! A sentence!

(He moves with knife drawn toward Antonio.)

Come, prepare!

PORTIA: Wait a little. There's something else.
This bond gives you not one drop of
blood.
The exact words are "a pound of flesh."
So you may take your bond and your
pound of flesh.
But, if in cutting it, you shed one drop of
Christian blood, your lands and goods,

Under the laws of Venice, will be
Confiscated to the state of Venice.

SHYLOCK *(appalled)*: Is that the law?

PORTIA *(opening the lawbook)*: You can see
For yourself. You pressed for justice.
Be assured you shall have even more
Justice than you want.

GRATIANO: Oh, learned judge!

SHYLOCK: I take the offer then. Pay
Three times the bond, and let him go.

BASSANIO: Here's the money.

PORTIA *(raising her hand)*: Gently now!
The Jew shall have justice.
He shall have nothing but the penalty.

GRATIANO: Oh, upright, learned judge!

PORTIA: Therefore, prepare to cut the flesh.
Shed no blood. And cut neither less
Nor more than exactly one pound of flesh.
If you take more or less than one pound,
Even if by one twentieth of an ounce—
If the scale turns by so little as a hair—
Then you shall die, and all your goods
Will be confiscated.
Why do you pause? Take your forfeit.

SHYLOCK *(thwarted)*: Give me my money,
And let me go.

BASSANIO: I have it ready for you. Here it is.

PORTIA: He has refused it in open court.
He shall have strict justice and his bond.

SHYLOCK: Not even my money back?

PORTIA: You shall have nothing but the forfeit,
And that to be taken at your peril, Jew.

SHYLOCK: I'll stand for no more of this!

(He turns to leave.)

PORTIA: Wait a moment, Jew.
The law has yet another hold on you.

(She consults the lawbook again.)

It is a law of Venice that if it is proved
Against an alien that he directly
Or indirectly seeks the life of any citizen,
The person against whom he plots
Can seize one half of his goods.
The other half goes to the state treasury.
The life of the offender lies only at the
Mercy of the duke.

(She closes the book.)

It appears from your actions that indirectly,
And directly too, you have plotted against
The very life of the defendant. You are
Indeed in danger of the death penalty.
Down on your knees, therefore,
And beg for the duke's mercy.

DUKE: To show the difference in our spirits,

I pardon your life before you ask for it.
Half your wealth goes to Antonio.
The other half goes to the state.
Your contrition could turn this to a fine.

PORTIA: Yes, the state's half. Not Antonio's.

SHYLOCK: No, take my life as well!
Don't pardon that. You take my house,
When you remove my source of income.
You take my life when you take away
The means by which I earn a living.

PORTIA: What mercy can you offer, Antonio?

ANTONIO: I would be pleased if the court
Were willing to give up the state's half,
And let me have the other half to use
During his lifetime. After that, I'll give it
To the gentleman who recently eloped with
His daughter. Two more conditions.
  One: In exchange for this favor,
He shall become a Christian immediately.
Two: That he makes a will here in court,
Leaving all he possesses at his death
To his son-in-law Lorenzo and his
  daughter.

DUKE: Very well. He shall do this—or I will
  take back
The pardon that I have just pronounced!

PORTIA: Do you agree, Jew?

SHYLOCK: I agree.

PORTIA *(to Nerissa)*: Clerk, draw up a will.

SHYLOCK: Please, give me permission to go.
I am not well. Send the will after me,
And I will sign it.

DUKE: You may leave, but see you do it!

(Shylock exits, a broken man.)

Antonio, reward this young man.
I think you are greatly indebted to him.

(The duke and his attendants leave.)

BASSANIO *(to Portia)*: My good sir,
My friend and I have been spared
Grave penalties because of your wisdom.
We gladly give you the 3,000 ducats
That were due to the Jew.

ANTONIO: And, in love and gratitude,
We stand indebted to you
Far more than that, forevermore.

PORTIA *(refusing the money)*: He is well-paid
Who is well-satisfied. And in saving you,
I am satisfied. Therefore, I count myself
Well-paid. *(bowing)* Pray, remember me
When we meet again.

(She starts to leave.)

BASSANIO *(stopping her)*: Dear sir, I must
Ask you again to take some souvenir of us
As a gesture, not as a fee.

Grant me two things, I beg you.
Pardon my persistence, and don't say no.

PORTIA: You press me hard, so I'll give in.
Give me your gloves. I'll wear them
For your sake.

(Bassanio removes them.)

And, in token of your love,
I'll take this ring from you.

(Bassanio withdraws his hand sharply.)

Don't draw back your hand.
Surely you shall not deny me this?

BASSANIO: But this ring, good sir—
Alas, it is a trifle.
I would not shame myself to give it to you.

PORTIA: I will have nothing else but this ring.
I've taken a fancy to it.

BASSANIO: This ring is more important to me
Than its value. I will give you
The most valuable ring in Venice,
And I'll find it by advertising for it.
With respect, you must pardon me for this.

PORTIA: I see, sir, you are generous in offers.
First you taught me how to beg, and now
You teach me how a beggar
Should be answered.

BASSANIO: Good sir, this ring was given to me
By my wife. When she put it on my hand,

She made me vow that I should
Neither sell it, nor give it away, nor lose it.

PORTIA: That's an excuse many men use to
Keep their gifts. If your wife knew
How well I deserve this ring, she would
Not stay angry with you for giving
It to me. Well, peace be with you!

*(**She** leaves, followed by **Nerissa**.)*

ANTONIO *(distressed)*: Lord Bassanio,
Let him have the ring.
Weigh his worthiness and my love
Against your wife's commandment!

BASSANIO *(giving in)*: Go, Gratiano.
Run and catch him. Give him the ring.
Go quickly!

*(**Gratiano** hurries off.)*

(to Antonio): Come. Let's go and rest.
Early in the morning we'll go to Belmont.

*(**They** leave together.)*

| Scene 2 |

*A street outside the law courts in Venice. **Portia** and **Nerissa** enter.*

PORTIA *(giving a paper to Nerissa)*: Ask the way to
the Jew's house.

Give him this, and have him sign it.
We'll leave tonight and be home a day
Before our husbands get there.
Lorenzo will be glad to get this will.

(Gratiano enters, breathless from running.)

GRATIANO: Finally, I've caught up with you.
My Lord Bassanio has sent you this ring.

PORTIA: I accept his ring most thankfully.
Please tell him so. One more thing!
Please show my clerk old Shylock's house.

GRATIANO: I'll do that.

NERISSA *(to Portia):* Sir, a word with you.
(She takes Portia aside.) I'll see if
I can get my husband's ring—the one
he swore to keep forever!

PORTIA: You can, I'm sure. No doubt they'll
Swear they gave the rings away to men!
But we'll stand up to them—
And outswear them, too. Now hurry!
You know where I'll be waiting.

(Portia leaves.)

NERISSA *(to Gratiano):* Come, good sir.
Will you show me to his house?

(They leave in the direction of Shylock's house.)

ACT 5

| Scene 1 |

Lorenzo and Jessica are in the garden of Portia's house in Belmont. It is a moonlit summer night. Stephano, Portia's servant, comes running up, followed by Lancelot, Bassanio's servant.

STEPHANO: Hello! Where's Master Lorenzo?

LORENZO: Stop yelling, man! Here I am.

STEPHANO: A messenger has come with
  News. My mistress will be here by
    morning.

LANCELOT: And my master is also on his way.

(Lancelot leaves.)

LORENZO: Dearest, let's go in and prepare
  For their arrival. And yet—why?
  Why should we go in?
  (to Stephano): My friend Stephano, please
    tell those
  In the house that your mistress is nearby,
  And then bring the musicians out.

(Stephano goes indoors.)

  How sweetly the moonlight sleeps here!
  We will sit, and let the sounds of music

Fall gently on our ears. Look, Jessica,
See how the night sky is dotted
With tiles of bright gold. Even the smallest
Star sings in his movements
Like an angel sings in a choir.
Such harmony is also in immortal souls.
But while we are in our mortal bodies,
We cannot hear it.

*(**Musicians** come out and disappear among the trees.*
***Lorenzo** calls out to them.)*

Begin, then. With soft chords,
Reach your mistress's ear,
And draw her home with music.
(to Jessica): Listen to the music!

*(Music plays. **Portia** and **Nerissa** enter.)*

PORTIA *(looking toward the house)*: That light
We see is burning in my hallway.
How far that little candle throws its beams!
So shines a good deed in a wicked world.

NERISSA: When the moon shone,
We didn't see the candle.

PORTIA: That's because greater powers
Dim the lesser. A stand-in looks as regal
As a king until the real king comes by.
Then his importance lessens, like an
Inland brook does when it reaches the sea.
(She listens.) Music! Listen!

87

NERISSA: They are your own musicians,
  Coming from your house.

PORTIA: How important the setting is!
  I think it sounds much sweeter than by day.

NERISSA: The silence improves it, madam.

PORTIA: The crow sings as sweetly as the lark
  When no one is listening. If a nightingale
  Sang by day, when every barnyard fowl
  Is cackling, would it be thought
    no better a musician than the wren?
  How many things sound better
  In the right season and at the right time!
  Quiet now! The moon rests behind a
    cloud,
  And does not want to be awakened.

(The music stops as the light fades.)

LORENZO: Oh! That is the voice—
  Or I am much mistaken—of Portia!

PORTIA: You know me as the blind man
  Knows the cuckoo—by the bad voice.

LORENZO: Dear lady, welcome home!

PORTIA: We've been praying for the welfare
  Of our husbands. Have they returned yet?

LORENZO: No, madam, not yet.
  But a messenger said they are on their way.

PORTIA: Go in, Nerissa. Tell my servants

Not to mention that we were gone.
Nor must you, Lorenzo. Jessica, nor you!

(A trumpet sounds, announcing Bassanio.)

LORENZO: Your husband is nearby. *(winking)*
We are not telltales, madam. Fear not.

(The cloud passes by. The scene is moonlit again.)

PORTIA: This night seems more like daylight
When it is sick. It looks a little paler—
Like a day when the sun is hidden.

*(**Bassanio, Antonio, Gratiano,** and their **followers** arrive. **Gratiano** and **Nerissa** stand aside and talk separately.)*

PORTIA: Welcome home, my lord.

BASSANIO: Thank you, madam.
Welcome my friend, too. Here is the man—
This is Antonio—to whom I owe so much.

PORTIA: You should feel deeply honored.
I hear he nearly paid a great debt for you.

ANTONIO: No more than I was glad to pay.

PORTIA: You are very welcome to our home.

GRATIANO *(to Nerissa, as they have been arguing about the ring)*: By the moon above,
I swear you are wrong! Honestly,
I gave it to the judge's clerk.
May he lose his manhood for all I care,
Since you take it so much to heart, my love!

PORTIA *(overhearing)***:** A quarrel already?
  What's the matter?

GRATIANO: It's about a hoop of gold,
  A paltry ring she gave me. It had words
  Engraved on it: "Love me. Leave me not."

NERISSA: Why talk about the words on it
  Or the value of it? You swore to
  Wear it until the hour of your death! You
  Said it would lie with you in your grave.
  For the sake of your passionate oaths,
  You should have kept it.
  Gave it to a judge's clerk! How well I know
  That the clerk will never have a beard!

GRATIANO: He will, if he lives to be a man.

NERISSA: Yes, if a woman lives to be a man!

GRATIANO: On my honor! I gave it to a youth,
  A kind of boy. A little, well-scrubbed boy,
  No taller than you. He begged it as a fee.
  I could not for all my heart deny it to him.

PORTIA: You were to blame. I must be frank.
  To part so lightly with your wife's first gift!
  I gave my love a ring, and made him swear
  Never to part with it, and here he stands—
  I'll vouch that he would not leave it,
  Or pull it from his finger, for all the wealth
  In the world. Now truly, Gratiano,
  You've caused your wife some grief,
  And if it were me, I'd be angry about it.

BASSANIO *(aside)*: I'd better cut my left hand
　Off and swear I lost the ring defending it.

GRATIANO: Lord Bassanio gave his ring to the
　Judge who begged it from him. He
　Indeed deserved it, too. Then his clerk,
　Who took so much trouble with the papers,
　Begged for mine. Neither clerk nor
　Judge would take anything but the rings.

PORTIA: Which ring did you give, my lord?
　Not the one you got from me, I hope.

BASSANIO: If I could add a lie to a fault,
　I would deny it. But you can see my finger
　Does not have the ring on it. It is gone.

PORTIA *(turning away)***:** And your false heart
Is just as empty of the truth! By heaven,
I will not sleep with you until I see the ring.

NERISSA *(to Gratiano)***:** Nor will I sleep with
you, Gratiano, until I see my ring again.

BASSANIO: Sweet Portia! If you knew
To whom, for whom, and why I gave it,
You wouldn't be so angry!

PORTIA: If you had known the ring's meaning,
Or half the worthiness of she who gave it,
Or your own duty to keep it,
You would never have parted with it!
No man would be so unreasonable as to
Insist on an item of such sentimental value.
Nerissa has the right idea. Upon my life,
Some woman has that ring!

BASSANIO: On my honor, madam, no woman
Has it. I gave it to a judge who refused
3,000 ducats from me and begged
For the ring. At first, I denied him—
Even though he had saved the very life of
My dear friend! Sweet lady, what can I say?
I was forced to send it after him.
Filled with shame, I owed him a courtesy.
My honor would not be smeared
By such ingratitude. Pardon me, good lady.
By all these stars, if you had been there,
I think you would have begged me to

Give the ring to the worthy judge.

PORTIA: Let that judge never come near me!
But since he has the jewel that I loved
And that you swore to keep for me,
I will be as generous as you.
I'll not deny him anything I have—
Not my body nor my husband's bed.
I shall know him, I am sure of it.
If I'm left alone, by my honor—
Which is mine to give—I'll have that
Judge for a bedfellow!

NERISSA: And I'll have his clerk! Therefore,
Be careful not to leave me alone!

GRATIANO: Well, go on then. But don't let me
Catch him, for if I do, I'll—

ANTONIO *(interrupting)***:** How sad that I am the
Unhappy subject of these quarrels.

PORTIA: Please, sir, don't you worry.
You are welcome anyway.

BASSANIO: Portia, forgive me this wrong,
Which was forced on me. With our friends
As witnesses, I swear to you that
I will never break another oath!

ANTONIO: I once loaned my body to obtain
His happiness. But if not for the man
Who has your ring, I'd have lost my life.
Now I'll dare to be the guarantor again,

THE MERCHANT OF VENICE

With my soul as forfeit,
I swear that your husband
Will never again break faith with you.

PORTIA: Then you shall be his guarantor.
(taking off the ring) Give him this,
And tell him to keep it better than the
other.

ANTONIO: Here, Lord Bassanio,
Swear to keep this ring.

BASSANIO: By heaven, it is the same one
I gave to the judge.

PORTIA: I got it from him.
Forgive me, Bassanio. In return
For this ring, the judge slept with me.

NERISSA *(also showing a ring)*: And
Forgive me, gentle Gratiano.
That boy, the judge's clerk, lay with me
Last night on payment of this ring.

GRATIANO: What—are our wives unfaithful
Before we have deserved it?

PORTIA: Don't speak so grossly.
(She decides to explain.) Here is a letter.
It's from Bellario in Padua.
In it you will learn that
Portia was the judge and Nerissa her clerk.
Lorenzo can say that I left soon after you,
And just now returned. I have not yet

Entered my house. Antonio, welcome!
I have better news in store for you
Than you expect. *(She produces another*
letter.)
Read this. It says that three of your
Ships unexpectedly reached safe harbor.
How I stumbled on this letter is a secret.

ANTONIO: What? I'm speechless!

BASSANIO *(to Portia)*: Were you the judge,
And I didn't know you?

GRATIANO *(to Nerissa)*: Were you the clerk
Who fancied an affair behind my back?

NERISSA: Yes, but the clerk never means to
Do it—unless he lives to be a man!

BASSANIO *(to Portia)*: Sweet judge,
You shall sleep with me! And when
I am away, then sleep with my wife.

ANTONIO *(after reading his letter)*:
Sweet lady, you have given me life
And a future. For now I know for certain
That my ships have safely come to port.

PORTIA: Well, now, Lorenzo,
My clerk has good news for you, too.

NERISSA: And I'll give it to him without a fee.

(She hands over the will she has prepared.)
Here I give to you and Jessica a special
Deed of gift from the rich Jew.

Upon his death, you will have all he owns.

LORENZO: Fair ladies, you drop manna—
Food from heaven—before starving
people!

PORTIA: It is almost morning.
I'm sure you haven't got the whole story.
Let us go in. You can ask questions there,
And we will answer all things honestly.

GRATIANO: Let's do that. The first question
That my Nerissa must answer is this:
Would she rather wait until tomorrow
night
Or go to bed now, when there are
Only two more hours until daylight?
If it were day, I would wish it dark,
So I'd be sleeping with the judge's clerk.
While I live, nothing will worry me more
Than the safekeeping of Nerissa's ring!

*(They **all** enter the house, arm in arm.)*